Tales from an Alien's Toe

WARNING: This publication contains words such as **poo**, **bum** and **fart**, which some pooey, farty adults may find offensive. Bum!

Also available:

A Load of New Nonsense

ISBN 978-0-9559975-0-1

written by Mike Lucas and published by Ginger Cat Publishing.

Tales from an Alien's Toe

Mike Lucas

A Ginger Cat Book

Stolen from a very **different** alien that bears no resemblance to the dead one in the first book. Adapted by Mike Lucas.

First edition 2008
First print 2008

1

ISBN 978-0-9559975-1-8

Visit the website and leave some feedback,
or send your poems:

www.gingercatpublishing.co.uk

Acknowledgement

Many thanks to the Plym Family Robinson for their kind help and advice.
And to the boy who gave me a massive egg on my head one Hallowe'en when I was thirteen. That was when all the strange thoughts began…

Dedicated to Becky -
And you know it!

If newspapers reported all of the good things that happened in the world each day
They would be thicker than telephone directories…

What's in it...

'Monster' Poems

These poems are all about monsters -
All furry with big, pointy teeth.
There are all kinds of monsters within them,
Except for my favourite one, Keith.

The monsters' day out

Have you ever wondered what happened
To the monsters I found in the road,
And brought home for dinner at my house
On that night that was unusually cold?

As I mentioned I woke in the morning,
The dream like a cloud in my head,
Only to find them there with me,
And asking for breakfast in bed.

Well, they must have unpacked all the shopping
(And, as you know, I had bought plenty).
I was grateful they'd filled up the cupboards,
But the packets and boxes were empty.

Whilst the boot knocked me stone cold unconscious,
They must have all carried me in,
And then eaten the food I had bought them,
And mistaken the store for a bin.

So there I was stuck with four Schmoogles,
Accompanying ten Ignaroo,
And finishing off with twelve Grinsters,
With nothing for monsters to do.

I brushed my teeth while I was thinking
And got dressed outside of the door,
And when I got back in my bedroom,
I found there were eight monsters more.

There weren't any other new species:
No Spingles or Quinkers or Splots.
But bouncing around on my mattress
Were eight newly born monster tots.

I said to the proud monster ladies,
"I didn't know you were pregnant last night."
The ladies looked down at their nine legs,
And said, "We were not - you are right."

But that subject I didn't wish to dwell on -
An idea had just come to my mind.
The fairground had opened that morning
And the weather was looking divine.

I promised them food when we got there,
And we all walked out into the day.
A Grinster spoke to me in Monstrish,
And asked if it was a long way.

I explained that it wasn't much further
Than the journey we'd take to come back,
And he said if it took any longer
He would have Schmoogle tot as a snack.

So they bundled back into my small car -
Their manners were slightly uncouth.
But we couldn't fit in all the Grinsters,
So the baby ones went on the roof.

I'm not boring you all with the journey
(I did that in rhyme number one).
Needless to say it was crowded,
And I wanted it over and done.

So we arrived at the fairground at lunchtime
And I unstrapped the kids from the top,
But one of them couldn't help crying,
"I was scared and I wanted to stop!"

Then the rest of the monsters exploded
From the doors of my car once again,
And this time they were so tightly packed in
That they popped like a cork from champagne.

The first thing to do was to feed them,
And I said, "There'll be hot dogs all round!"
And the next thing I knew Mummy Schmoogle
Was setting alight a poor hound.

It was too late to save the old dog now,
So I dragged them away to the tent.
Then I ordered up seventy hot dogs,
And this time they knew what I meant.

And then there were seventy burgers,
And seventy candy floss too,
And seventy toffee bananas,
And seventy trips to the loo.

And then they all said they were thirsty
So I bought seventy bottles of pop.
But they just tried to squirt one another,
So I told them quite sternly to stop.

And then it was time for the fun bit.
We queued for an hour for the wheel.
It took us around in ten seconds,
And a Grinster brought up his whole meal.

So we thought we would go on the dodgems,
But the Ignaroo didn't understand -
You were meant to crash into each other -
And demanded all children be banned.

Then we walked to the mirrors of magic,
That distorted all shapes, short and tall,
And made humans look just like the Schmoogles.
So the Schmoogles adopted them all,

And took them all onto the ghost train
Which broke down very near to the end.
When the engineer came in they jumped out
From the ghost he was trying to mend.

The coconut shy man was cheating -
That nut was just too hard to hit.
So a Schmoogle got into a tantrum
And threw a small Grinster at it.

He won a big teddy as jackpot,
And cuddled it sweetly, then said,
"I'll share it," and ripped it to pieces,
Then put his hand inside its head.

"*I'm just a small teddy, don't eat me*!"
The monsters all fell on the floor,
And laughed at the joke with the teddy,
Then asked if they could eat one more.

I said, "We must really be going.
The babies are closing their eyes."
But the Ignaroo Mum said, "Don't worry.
We'll just give them away as a prize."

So that's what they did with the babies -
To people who wanted to play,
They could guess the new names for the monsters
And the winner could take them away.

We had Ian and Martin and Dave and Juan Carlos
And Chloe, Charmaine and Chantelle.
But we thought Quasimodo was what we liked best
Because, somehow, that name rang a bell.

So we gave all the babies away to a lady
Who'd already won a huge frog.
And I saw in the distance an angry old man,
And beside him a smouldering dog.

So I said to the monsters, "Look lively!
It's time that we really did split."
But, with all of the food they had eaten,
In the car there was no way they'd fit.

So some Ignaroo climbed in the front seat,
And some Schmoogles climbed into the back.
Grinsters half in the boot, and the rest on the roof,
And the car full of creaks and of cracks...

In the mirror I saw the man pointing,
So I screamed to the monsters, "Hang on!"
And before they replied we were moving.
And before he arrived we were gone.

As we disappeared over the mountain,
And we headed back home to Chez Me,
A small Schmoogle leaned over my shoulder,
And asked, "Mister, what time is tea?"

The monster under the bed

Always keep your feet hidden underneath the sheets,
And you'll sleep as safe as houses every night.
But never let your toes escape the duvet or, who knows,
The monster underneath might take a bite.

He waits there whilst you're sleeping, but disappears when you go
peeping -
He turns himself invisible and hides.
But don't you think he isn't there - as you'll discover if you dare
To let your foot fall out and drop over the side.

So, a word of good advice (and I'm not going to tell you twice) -
Always keep your duvet firmly on your feet.
For the beast below your bed is waiting only to be fed,
And you're the tasty meal he wants to eat.

The monster down the plughole

Sitting in the bath one night
I saw a single bubble,
Rising up between my feet.
I thought, *Oh, here comes trouble.*

And then the plug shot out and up
And landed on the floor,
And a finger poked up through the hole,
And then one finger more.

I reached down for the fingers
And I gave them both a yank,
And out came a small monster
Who said, "Thanks - I nearly sank."

I asked what he was doing
Down the plughole in my bath.
He said, "I'm here to scare you,"
And I couldn't help but laugh.

"You?" I said, "Scare me? Well,
How d'you intend to do that, chum?"
And then the monster dived down deep
And bit me on the bum.

"Yeeoow!" I yelled and jumped out quick,
"Why did you do that, pest?"
He said, "I am a monster
And that's what monsters do do best."

I wrapped a towel around myself
And looked him up and down.
The water rose up past his heads
So, to make sure he wouldn't drown,

I picked him up and held him close,
Then whispered in his ear,
"You cannot scare a person
Just by biting on his rear.

You see, scaring me and hurting me
Are not the same, you know."
And just to prove the point
I went and pulled off all his toes.

"Now that is hurting," I explained,
As the monster howled in pain.
"And now I'll show you scaring
And you'll see they're not the same."

So I put him on the bath tub
And I pulled my head clean off,
And held it by its severed throat,
Which I cleared with a small cough.

I pulled my ears off, pulled my eyes out,
Threw them in the bath,
And whispered to the monster, "Boo!"
And laughed an evil laugh.

And then I put my hand inside
And wrenched it out real quick,
And as my beating heart appeared
I heard him being sick.

So I put it all back into place,
And screwed my head back on.
I washed the soap out of my eyes,
And saw the monster gone.

Then I saw the plug pulled downwards,
And a single rising bubble.
I climbed back in and closed my eyes
And thought, *well, there goes trouble.*

How to get rid of a monster

If you see a monster while you're lying in your bed,
Make a funny face at him, then pat him on the head.
Sing a silly song and poke your tongue out as you do,
And tell him that your brother is much tastier than you.

Sick!

Quick! Quick!
Lickety split!
Dad stop the car
'Cause I'm going to be sick.
I can't hold it back -
I can taste it a bit.
Quick dad, I'm going to be sick!

Oh, no!
Geronimo!
Just breathe in deeply -
I'm going to go slow.
Swallow it down
And wind down the window.
Calm, son, I'm going to go slow.

Dad! Dad!
Ziggedy zag!
He's going all funny
And smells really bad.
A bit's coming out
Of his mouth - just a tad.
Oh, dad, he looks monstrously bad.

Tut! Tut!
Cluckety cluck!
I told you that human
Was not fully cooked.
Our baby's been poisoned
From eating that muck.
That human was not fully cooked.

There, there -
All monsters take care.
If you eat a human
You'd better beware.
Make sure it's well done
And not medium rare.
Monsters, you'd better beware.

Fluffy monsters

Never cross the zombie bunny -
He's not cute and it's not funny.
He'll come to you when you expect it least.

He's got a friend - the vampire kitty.
She's got sharp teeth and not too pretty.
But still she's not the most horrific beast.

And it's not the werewolf teddy,
With blood red eyes and furry belly,
Who scares me like the next one on the list.

For scaring, nobody can beat her.
She looks just like a P.E. teacher,
But everybody knows that she's a witch.

She makes you run until you ache,
Leaves broken children in her wake,
Takes no excuses for forgotten P.E. kit.

She rips up sick notes just for fun,
Gives out detentions one by one,
And smiles as children stumble, fall and trip.

So I have planned my sweet revenge
With all my fluffy, furry friends.
I'll give her back her, "One…two…ready…steady…"

I've sneaked them all into her desk
To do to her what they do best -
My undead bunny, kitty and my teddy!

My adopted monster

If I ever adopted a monster
He would have to be little and sweet,
With red rosy cheeks on his big chubby face
And pink podgy fingers and feet.
He would have to make gurgley noises,
And crawl round the room on all fours,
And laugh when I tickled his dimply chin,
And cry if he's ever ignored.
He would sometimes smell worse than school dinners,
And scream louder than kids in my class,
And sometimes be lovely and cuddly,
And sometimes a pain in the neck.
But wait - I've already adopted
A monster of similar ilk -
He's cuddling up to my mummy,
And drinking his bottle of milk.

There's a monster in my teacup

There's a monster in my teacup
And I don't know what to say -
The Vicar has two sugars
And the Mayor prefers Earl Grey.
But I really don't remember
Either of them telling me
They liked to take a little monster
In their cup of tea.

He's floating on the surface
And I've given it a stir,
But that monster's not dissolving,
Though he's lost most of his fur.
I've bopped him with my teaspoon
On his head to make him sink,
And now the Vicar's asking
If I'll be long with his drink.

I've tried to scoop him out
But he just doesn't want to come.
I've tried to pick him up
But he just snarls and bites my thumb.
The Mayor has asked for biscuits
And the Vicar's calling me.
I'm going to have to leave that monster
In the cup of tea.

I carry in the tray with
Cups and biscuits on a plate.
The monster gasps for air
But he is going to have to wait.
The Vicar smiles, the Mayor gives thanks
As I put down the tray.
And then the Vicar takes a cup
And asks us all to pray.

So as they close their eyes
I grab the cup of tea and then
I try to find the monster
Before the Vicar says, "Amen."
I dip my fingers in the cup
Of boiling water and
The monster screams, "Please save me!"
And then clamps onto my hand.

As I hop around the room in pain
The Vicar stops his prayer.
He opens up his eyes and wraps
His arms around the Mayor.
He screams, "It was Earl Grey for you,
And one sugar for me.
But I don't recall that either
Mentioned monsters in our tea!"

Ode to Trevor

Trevor's the monster who lives in our bin.
He used to be fat but he's now, oh, so thin.
I know that it's vital, but now we recycle
No rubbish is getting to him.

Trevor's upset 'cause we really don't care
For the plight of the millions of Trevors out there.
I know it's our planet, but Trevor's a gannet -
To ignore him is really unfair.

So I'm begging you please just to stop and think twice -
To be nice to Trevor - to Trevor be nice.
Don't think purely green, but think aquamarine,
Or the extinction of Trevor's the price.

Giant pixie monster

I saw a giant pixie in the garden.
He was the biggest pixie that I ever saw.
As pixies go he really was a monster.
As giants go he really was quite small.

I saw a tiny giant in the garden.
He really was the shortest one around.
As giants go he really was the smallest
Of all the giants that I've ever found.

I saw an ugly monster in the garden.
He was sitting down and reading by the tree.
And my dad's the only person that I know of
Who matches the description of all three.

Monster shoes

Monster shoes
On my feet
I'm a monster
Human meat!

Monster shoes
Off my feet
Not a monster
Kind and sweet

Monster shoes
On at night
I'm a monster
Kids to bite

Monster shoes
Off at day
Big bad monster
Gone away

Shoe on left
Shoe off right
Not quite day
Not quite night

Confused monster
Nice but mean
Half a monster
In between

'Weird' Poems

These poems are really quite weird, you know.
I'd say they're as weird as a spoon in the snow.
And not just in snow, but in snow on the moon:
Bagpipe, banana, baboon.

But enough contemplating - my picnic was waiting.
I opened my lunchbox and ate.
Though the weather was pasty, my picnic was tasty,
And I smiled as I watched the sun set.

Then I thought of the locals - those stupid old yokels.
What nonsense they spoke with their warning.
Did they think me so gullible? That my legs were so pullable?
I would have my revenge in the morning.

Then a tiny sand hopper appeared on the top a'
My towel and I gave it a flick.
It flew back to the sand, lay there motionless and
I then finished it off with a kick.

Then another appeared and another, and more,
And I gazed all the way to the sea.
And the whole mass of beach, from the dunes to the reach,
Seemed to hop up and down towards me.

Well, I tried to get up, but my two feet were stuck,
And they seemed to be sinking down deeper.
Then I tried with my hands, but the weight of the sand
Stopped me lifting them too. Jeepers creepers!

Then the great hopping hulk swarmed all over my bulk:
Up my nose; in my mouth; in my hair.
There were thousands and millions (no - billions and trillions)
And I sank down to heaven knows where.

As the day turned to night, my life's last final sight
Was one hideous, evil and foul.
'Twas a giant sand hopper (oh, boy what a whopper!)
With Beryl and Cyril both riding on top a'
That beast with a grin and then fisherman Jim,
And then last, but not least, Simon Cowell.

A strange dream

Down in the cellar
With my broken umbrella -
There wasn't a raindrop in sight.
But a rainbow appeared,
Which was terribly weird,
For it was still the middle of night.
Then an alien said,
"Get back into your bed,
For you're having a dream and it's daft."
But I was stuck in that dream,
So I dreamt of a stream,
And I sailed back to bed on a raft.

How the cows disappeared

The cows began to vanish on the day the rats appeared.
Come to think of it, that was the day the men began to lose their beards.
And all the cats around the town began to cat walk upside down.
And spaghetti was forbidden, which I always thought quite weird.

I think it all began with the arrival of this foreign man
Who opened up a restaurant on the corner of my street.
His name was Juan Corletti and he made the best spaghetti
That you ever could have tasted, which I always thought quite neat.

But the pasty shop just down the road was not too happy, I was told.
The manager complained to all and sundry and the Mayor.
The Mayor (who loved a pasty and was pretty mean and nasty)
Went and shut down Juan Corletti, which I always thought unfair.

Now, never cross Italians, unless you don't mind a dead stallion
Lying next to you in bed (go ask your dad - he'll understand).
Next the restaurateur said, "Bella! Now you're going to get it, fella!"
Then he threw him from the restaurant, which I always thought quite
grand.

Well, the Italian had a sister (because she lived abroad he missed her),
And he called her up to ask her if she'd like to come along.
His sister was a wicked witch, who had a truly evil itch
That needed scratching with some mischief, which I always thought quite
wrong.

All the townsfolk loved their cats, and there is nothing wrong with that:
The Mayor, himself, he had a dozen and his wife a dozen more.
But the owners spoilt them rotten, and they wrapped them up in cotton
Wool and treated them like royals, which I always thought quite poor.

To seek revenge upon the town, she turned the pussies upside down
And made them walk upon the ceilings with their feet up in the air.
The blood rushed straight to their heads and one by one they all dropped dead,
And Juan Corletti and his sister laughed, which I always thought quite rare.

It was customary here to grow your whiskers from your ears
Down to your chin and never shave (and it was just the same for men).
It was quite a sight to see these - all these hairy beardy weirdies -
But one day their whiskers all fell out, which I thought was weird again.

It was all due to the sister of that old Italian mister -
She had cast another spell upon the people within range.
And bare faces then appeared. They all felt naked without beards,
So they all ran into hiding, which I always thought quite strange.

As the people left a gap within that town upon the map,
And the cats all died, the rats began to creep out of their holes.
And the town was overrun with tiny mammals having fun:
Rats and mice and little blind things, which I always thought were voles.

So Juan Corletti won the day in the most extraordinary way,
And he served up his spaghetti to the rodents in the town.
And, the witch, she moved back home to a small village near to Rome.
And the townsfolk stayed in hiding, but I always stayed around.

So I'm sitting on my tractor after writing all these chapters
Filled with random things I never would have made up if I could:
The spaghetti and the cats, beardy-weirdies and the rats.
But where the cows all went to I have never understood.

The lady witches' freestyle diving

The lady witches' freestyle diving
Was ruined by petty conniving…

Off the board the first witch flew,
Whilst sipping still her witch's brew,
And did a backward somersault,
Then disappeared - 'Twas her own fault
For, whilst concocting her new potion,
She misread a simple caution
Which stated, '*Do not bend the knees*
Whilst diving, or you'll turn to cheese.'
There sounded but a single *PLOP!*
As the cheddar did a belly flop.

All the witches laughed and cheered
When that first witch disappeared.

The next on was a nasty hag -
A member of the WIZARDS' WAGS.
The rules were clear - no brooms permitted -
But, not one to be outwitted,
She sprinkled bat poo on her broom
Whilst in her mystic changing room.
Enchanted bat poo has the gift
Of granting one the broom's own lift.
It has another gift, I've found,
Of attracting all the bats around.
That wicked witch found out that truth
Whilst smashing wildly through the roof.

The other witches howled and whooped
As she was coated in bat poop.

The third on made a real big splash,
No doubt caused by her moustache.
She'd heard that shaving all her hair
Would make her faster through the air.
But the thing you shouldn't cause a witch
Is unscratchable razor's itch.
She'd had to jump into a bath
Of tiny hair-growing giraffes.
But, as she left the diving board,
Hair sprouted faster than it ought.

The witch spectators mocked and joked
As they, by a tidal wave, were soaked.

The last dive of complexity,
(Of witchful synchronicity)
A dozen witches in a row,
With nowhere but downwards to go.
No cheating or depravity -
Purely the force of gravity.
One, two, three, a perfect start -
Twelve hags in pure performing art.
A backward flip, a forward twist
Without a deed done devilish.
In perfect time, with perfect focus -
Not one witch uses hocus-pocus.

Half way down and looking good
And diving as a diver should.

But, however, in their pews,
The watching witches aren't amused.
This isn't what they came here for
(Not cheating's one thing they abhor)

And all stand up and cast a spell,
"Oh, demons waiting down in hell…
Oh, you who have been truly cursed…
Open the ground and quench your thirst!"
And, faster than the speed of sound,
The water in the pool goes down
To leave a concrete floor below
Twelve perfectly posed forward rolls.
They haven't got the time to stop,
Or magic spells to take them up,
And so they meet their sudden ends
As judging witches give them 10's.

The audience flies out the rear
And cackles, "Same again next year!"

Trees

At a quarter to five all the trees come alive
In the forest outside my front door.
Needless to say, when I go out to play,
I am back home by four forty four.

I can hear them all screaming whilst I am in dreaming -
They continue on all through the night.
And I wake without rest, with an urge to protest
That their bark isn't worse than their bite.

Zee mad prawfessah

I ist zee mad prawfessah
Und I'll tell you vhy eez zees -
I tvied to make ein monstah
From zee body off ein feesh.
I kutz heez head awff viz ein kuh-nife
Und throwed avay heez tail,
Und joint eet to ein sqvirrel's head
Veez ein seex eench rhusty nail.
I gotzed ein froggy's vebbedd feetz
Und glued zem on zee back;
Ein kvabby's beeg frunt peenzers
Vhich I shticked veez shticky tack.
He veally voz ein monstah.
"Ja, du ist mad!" I heers vun say.
Buht I ist only mad becawse
Zat monstah hopt avay!

Alien in my brain

Oh, my gosh! There's an alien in my brain.
It crawled inside my ear today and hasn't come out again.
It flew through space onto my face.
It's driving me insane.
Oh, my gosh! Get that alien out of my brain.

Oh, my gosh! There's an alien on my toe.
It's taking me to places that I really don't want to go.
It hopped down there from who knows where.
What next? I do not know.
Oh, my gosh! Get that alien off my toe.

Oh, my gosh! There's an alien up my nose.
It tried to hide and flew inside when I kicked up my toes.
What can I do? I sneezed, I blew.
I'm stuck with it, I s'pose.
Oh, my gosh! Get that alien down from my nose.

Oh, my gosh! There's an alien in my belly.
It's pushing on my button and it's turned my legs to jelly.
I hope I don't (I'm sure I won't)
End up like that man on the telly.
Oh, my gosh! Get that alien out of my belly.

Oh, my gosh! There's an alien up my bum.
I don't know where it's heading, but I know where it came from -
He's travelled south from near my mouth
And passed right through my tum.
Oh, my gosh! Get that alien out of my bum.

Oh, my gosh! There's an alien down my loo.
He came out of my bottom and I know just what to do.
He'll have to stay that stinky way,
From heads to foot in poo.
Pull the flush! Send that alien down the loo!

In space nobody eats salad cream

They all looked like giant cucumbers,
But they came from a world far away
To take over the bodies of people,
And on Earth for forever to stay.

But the Earthlings thought something suspicious,
And fought back the invasion so cruel,
When six foot two-legged cucumbers
Showed up at their work and their school.

The Prime Minister went on the telly
To dismiss what the people had seen,
But he was obviously not to be trusted
As he stood there too long and too green.

They attack when their victims are sleeping,
And no-one's escaped from them yet.
But one woke up half way through changing,
And turned into a three foot courgette.

There is only one known way to kill them
And, it's true, we have tried many ways -
You must catch them and slice them and dice them,
And then cover them in mayonnaise.

The human race never recovered.
There's nobody left here but me.
And the irony of the whole story
Is I'm having a salad for tea.

My sofa

The sofa was delivered on the eve of Hallowe'en.
I opened up the front door - there was no-one to be seen.
I put it in my living room beside the open fire.
And I wondered who had ordered it. Who was the mystery buyer?

That evening as the wind howled, and the rain lashed at my door,
I settled down to watch TV, but sat upon the floor.
I couldn't bring myself to sit upon that mystery couch.
My eyes began to close and I began to droop and slouch.

I was awoken by some sounds: a growl, a scraping and a whine.
I opened up my eyes and felt a chill run down my spine.
I cast my eyes around the room, so shocked at what I saw.
My furniture was missing. There was sawdust on the floor.

And then I turned towards the noise; the chewing (oh, the fear),
And saw my sofa munching on a table from IKEA.
It finished off and coughed a cough, then spat a caster out,
Which hit my hanging lamp and caused the lights to sway about.

I could hear the sofa shuffling slow along the fitted rug.
It sucked it out from under me with such a forceful tug
That I nearly went along with it into that sofa's jaws,
But I scrambled up hysterically without a moment's pause.

The last thing I remember as I headed for the door
Was the squeak of rusty casters as it rolled along the floor.
I ran outside to try and hide and gulped in the fresh air,
And then was gobbled up by my new sofa's matching chair.

Bug in a raindrop

In every raindrop there may be
A little bug too small to see,
And every time he rains on me
I get a little wet.

I'm waiting here to catch that bug
And put him in this plastic jug,
And hear him going, *glug! glug! glug!*
And keep him as a pet.

Here comes a bug above my head,
Inside a raindrop, like I said.
Oh dear, he's hit the floor - he's dead.
He fell right through my net.

And then the rain begins to pour.
I try to catch it like before.
What do they live in raindrops for?
I'll go and ask my vet.

"Please, Mr. Vet, answer me why
Bugs live in raindrops in the sky,
Then fall to Earth where they all die.
What is the thrill they get?"

But Mr. Vet just looked at me
And said, "Young man can you not see?
Those little bugs don't fall at all,
But fly their little jets.

They also wear a special suit
So, when they pull their parachutes,
Their little bodies, small and cute,
Will not get cold and fret.

They live on clouds and fly to Earth,
Where lady bugs can then give birth
To baby bugs who bring such mirth,
But place them deep in debt.

And that is why they cannot stay,
But quickly grow, then float away
To clouds where they work night and day
To build their own small jet.

The bugs break forth - that's condensation.
Fly to Earth - precipitation.
Give birth and rise - evaporation.
Do you have it yet?"

I thanked him and, my mind placated,
Went back home and contemplated
What the vet had just narrated,
And set free my small pet.

The bug cycle goes round and round
With bugs in raindrops falling down.
They do not die; they do not drown.
They don't even get wet.

So next time when you see the rain,
And see it gurgling down the drain,
Just look for lots of little planes.
I bet you'll net a jet.

Jack-in-the-box

I do not like my Jack-in-the-box,
For when I'm not looking he steals all my socks.
He takes them inside to another dimension
Where socks are subjected to things I can't mention.
They're worn at the heels and they're turned inside out.
They get hot and sweaty and smell like dead trout.
They're mixed and they're matched and are lost down the back
Of cupboards and drawers and shoved deep down the cracks.
They lose their free will and are there just to serve,
And don't ever get the respect they deserve.
My mum always asks me what happens to socks,
But I'm too scared to mention my Jack-in-the-box
For, to swear me to silence, he's left nothing to chance -
He's taken as hostage my favourite pants.

Zombie vampire frogs from outer space

What can I say? They arrived here one day
From a planet south west of the Skimmed-Milky Way.
They came in pyjamas, each riding space llamas,
And threatened us all with their loaded bananas.

They all spoke Chinese and ate fresh garden peas,
And when they passed lampposts would let out a sneeze.
So we built lampposts here and we built lampposts there.
As time passed we built lampposts everywhere.

We built them in shops and below sudden drops.
We built them where circles appeared in the crops.
We built them in pools and in primary schools,
And in castles where princesses kept all their jewels.

We built them on stages (and that took us ages).
We built them on wheels for the hamsters in cages.
We built them on bridges, in forests with midges,
And replaced all the lamps in the ovens and fridges.

So, as you can see, if you've listened to me,
We built them wherever a lamppost could be.
And the visitors passed them whilst eating their peas.
As they passed underneath they let out a great sneeze,

And then a great cough and their noses fell off
And, though it seems mean, all us humans did scoff.
See, their noses were where their three hearts were positioned -
Without their three hearts they were in no condition

To take over the Earth with their funny old ways
Of chewing on worms and of juggling on sleighs;
Of copying ducks and of licking old books
And staring through windows with curious looks;

Of playing space bingo and talking weird lingo;
Of going to clubs but refusing to mingle;
Of breaking up phones with old dinosaur bones
And of singing songs backwards in old people's homes.

And with no hearts inside our new visitors died
And, I have to admit, one or two of us cried.
But that's how and why we got rid of that race
Of strange zombie vampire frogs from outer space.

Frightened cushion

I like to hide behind a soft cushion
When a scary film is on T.V.
But the film that is on is so frightening
That the cushion has hid behind me.

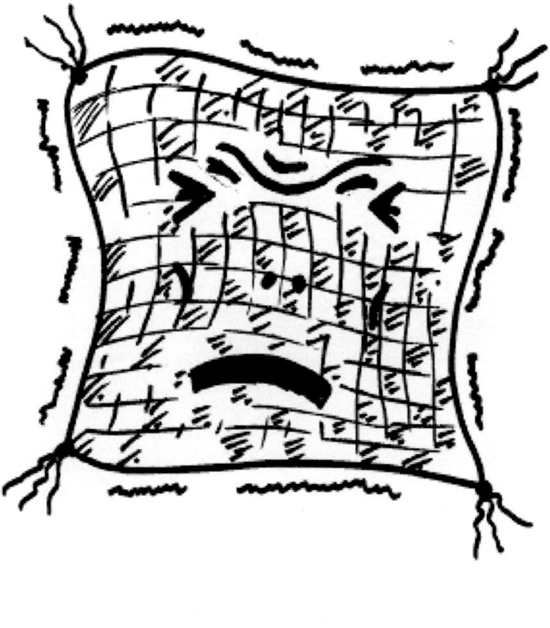

Anne the Gnome

My name is Anne the gnome
And this is my garden home.
I used to live here happy by myself.
I'd sit alone and fish
As was my only gnomey wish,
Until I had a visit from that poison elf.

Now, you may well think it strange
That Anne the Gnome's my real name,
Especially when you see my big long beard.
But I think it was that bloke
Who finds it quite a funny joke
To give his pet gnomes names which are quite weird.

There's been Maureen, Mary, Molly,
Deborah, Dorian and Dolly,
Kelly, Kerry, Shelley, Sherry, Betty, Bee.
There's been Brittany and Bella,
Stacey, Stephanie and Stella,
But Anne's the lady's name that he gave me.

Anyway, that horrid elf
Saw me there all by myself,
And so he slowly sneaked up on me while I slept.
He put me in a sack
And then he carried me out back
To dump me where that bloke's old junk was kept.

The bin men came and took me.
Well, I guess that they mistook me
For a smelly bit of rubbish from the pile.
And they drove me to the tip

And tipped me headfirst into it,
Where I stayed there in the darkness for a while.

When I woke I felt for certain
That, for me, the gnomey curtain
Had been closed and I'd been sent to gnomey hell.
Then I heard a distant sound
Of someone digging underground,
And I was pulled up like a bucket from a well.

I saw the darkness ripped away
And felt the warmth of a new day,
And a familiar face gazed down at me in tears.
It was my owner, Funny Bloke,
Who'd named me Anne as a bad joke,
Of which I'd had to bear the brunt these many years.

I heard the bin men beg his pardon
As I was brought home to the garden
Where that nasty elf had thrown me in that sack.
Then he placed me in my spot
Where I stood working on a plot
To seek revenge upon the elf when he came back.

It was a little after ten
When evil elfy struck again.
I could hear his impious laugh as he drew near.
He was the scariest thing I'd seen,
A tiny devil dressed in green,
And by the smell of him he'd been out on the beer.

My eyes were almost closed,
And I was faking a gnome dose,
As he sneaked up with a grin and his big sack.
But as he readied for a strike
I leaned and spoke into my mike,
And all my other gnomey friends launched their attack.

There was Maureen, Mary, Molly,
Deborah, Dorian and Dolly,
Kelly, Kerry, Shelley, Sherry, Betty, Bee.
There was Brittany and Bella,
Stacey, Stephanie and Stella,
But Anne was at the front of it - that's me.

You see that man, who was my owner,
Knew about the elf (called Shona),
And he'd brought all of his gnomes out of retirement.
And we'd worked on our revenge,
Me and his other gnomey friends,
To stop that horrid elf from stealing my environment.

Well, that elf didn't know what hit him:
Eighteen gnomes and one small kitten,
Who had been waiting for a chance to catch a mouse.
And my friendly, jokey bloke
Watched as that nasty elf did croak,
Then took his gnomes and disappeared into the house.

Shona the Elf met a bad ending -
Elves are very good at bending
But if you pull one hard then they will snap.
And I hope you've learnt a lesson -
With garden gnomes don't you go messing,
Even if they look to be having a nap.

So that elf is gone forever
And my bloke, who is called Trevor,
Brought his gnome friends out so I'm not by myself.
And I still sit, rod in hand,
With a sign reading GNOME ANNE'S LAND
And, on top of that, at least I got my elf.

'Animal' Poems

These poems are not very scary,
But all are about beasts so hairy.
Well, one is all scaly,
And one is all snaily.
But none of them is ordinary.

Barry the Bat

Barry the Bat couldn't hang there like that -
Upside down in a cave full of others.
He liked his own space, and a bed's warm embrace,
As he snuggled down under the covers.

So he searched through the cave for some wood, and he made
Him a bed in his own quiet corner.
But Basher the Bat wasn't happy with that,
And much less when he saw Barry's sauna.

See, Basher and Barry had never been pally -
Basher was ugly and cruel.
He treated the bats like some furry doormats,
But Barry was nobody's fool.

He had guessed that that pest would cause batty unrest
When he noticed what Barry had done.
So he cooked up a plan (as he cooked up a flan
On his recently bought gas oven).

All of the rest really couldn't care less
And respected a bat's privacy.
They'd always liked Baz (just like I always has)
And, for them there was nothing to see.

But Basher just couldn't (well, he could, but he wouldn't)
Let Barry Bat lay there in peace.
So he sneaked up one night, soft and silent in flight,
As Baz lay in his sheets of cerise.

Now, the walls of that cave (Basher learnt this from Dave,
A professorial bat who was clever)
Were made of a stone which had one use alone -
To make fire when you rubbed it together.

So Basher slid forward (like a slug on a floor would),
Two rocks in his bat paws so tight.
The plan he had hatched with his primitive match
Was to set Barry Bat's bed alight.

It was just as the spark flew up out of the dark
That he noticed a smell strange and new.
And this smell he smelled last was the smell of some gas
Mingled in with the smell of bat poo.

Then a massive explosion, a batty commotion,
As Basher went **POOF!** in the dark.
And all the bats woke, shocked and choking on smoke,
And gazed down at a scorched bed shaped mark.

"Poor Barry is dead in his bed!" they all said.
"Oh, poor Barry did not deserve that.
So he liked his own space and a bed's warm embrace,
But that's no way to go for a bat."

Then out from his own private toilet alone
Staggered Barry the Bat, champion yawner.
The other bats cheered, "Barry Bat is still here!
But whose charcoaled wings in the corner?"

Barry stopped yawning whilst the others paused mourning,
Then stared at the wings on the floor.
"I fear Basher is gone for I left the gas on.
I repeat - I fear Basher's no more."

For a while nothing happened from inside that cavern,
Except for the buzzing of flies.
And Barry feared that all the upside down bats
Would blame him for mean Basher's demise.

But then one bat cried, "Here, let's give Barry three cheers!
For the evil bat, Basher is dead!"
And the others rejoiced in a unified voice,
"Let's help Barry Bat build a new bed!"

Max licks his bum

Max licks his bum,
But he's a cat.
I think that it's horrid
Doing that.
Max eats his food
Off the floor,
And stops a bit
To lick his bum some more.

The spider bully

Look at that cute little spider
Sitting alone on his web.
Look at the way that he's staring at me.
I think that I'll have me a leg.

Look at that seven legged spider
Searching around for his limb.
Look at the way that he's all on one side.
I'll take me another from him.

Look at that six legged spider
Wondering where his legs went.
If legs were like money for spiders,
Then here goes another one spent.

Look at that five legged spider
Trying to keep his legs on.
But I've got them hold pretty tightly.
Whoops! There's another one gone.

Look at that four legged spider
With half of his legs still alive,
The other half twitching and dying.
I think that I'll have number five.

Look at that three legged spider
Stumbling around on the floor.
Look at the five little legs in my hand.
I think that I'll have me one more.

Look at that two legged spider
Trying to balance upright.
He looks like he's walking a tightrope.
I think that I'll have me his right.

Look at that one legged spider
Circling around on the spot -
He looks like a small exclamation.
I think that I'll have me the lot.

Look at that no legged spider
With nothing to do but just sit.
I'm bored with this now but, before I go home,
I can't resist stepping on it.

Lonely tree on a hill

Lonely tree
On a hill
Squirrel climbs
Higher still

End of branch
Squirrel jumps
Squirrel falls
Squirrel bumps

Squirrel dead
Squirrel still.
Lonely tree
On a hill.

The snail

I was sitting in the garden when a snail came crawling by.
He was moving pretty slowly and his skin was cracked and dry.
It was a bright and sunny day with not a blade of grass for shade.
That poor old snail was burning up with every squirm he made.

I thought, *Oh, what a shame. I think I'll go and help you out.*
I know a way to cool you off. It'll only take about
A minute in the freezer and you'll feel as right as rain.
And when you're nice and cool I'll bring you back outside again.

So I picked him up and brought him in and placed him in the freezer.
I felt quite proud to think that I could help that little geezer.
I heard the phone begin to ring. I picked it up and then
I spoke for half an hour or so to my best friend called Ben.

I guess you know what happened. Do I have to spell it out?
That poor old snail was frozen stiff, of that there was no doubt.
So I popped him in the microwave to try and thaw him out.
And then the phone rang once again. What could this be about?

My next best friend, Belinda, said she'd phoned up for a chat.
We spoke for twenty minutes and I hung up after that.
As I went back to the kitchen I remembered that poor snail,
But there is a happy ending to this sad and tragic tale -
For I went and got a knife and fork, a plate and serviette.
And in the garden, with some garlic, that delicious snail I ate.

A man eating fish

I noticed a man eating fish on the beach
As I went out to look at the ships.
The man eating fish went and finished it off
And turned into a man eating chips.

Frightened giraffe

“You’re having a laugh,” said the frightened giraffe.
“I’m not going into that cave!
There could be a monster, a giraffe eating lobster,
An ogre who needs a new slave!

There could be a werewolf with terrible teeth,
Or a squirrel who carries an axe.
There could be a witch hiding in a dark ditch,
Or a vampire who waits…then attacks!

There could be a mummy awakened from sleep,
Or a ghost who likes blood for his tea.
There could be a bat who is trained in combat
And has got a mean grudge against me!

There could be a zombie who likes to eat brains,
Or a dragon with fiery breath.
There could be a mouse who’s as big as a house,
Or a snake who will crush me to death.

There could be a leech that will stick to my skin
And will grow to the size of a cow.
There could be a devil awaiting within -
I just know that there is, don’t ask how.

There could be a spider with babies inside her,
Who will swarm up my neck to my head.
There could be a rabbit just waiting to grab it
And squeeze it until I am dead.

There could be a yeti asleep on a settee
Just waiting for me to arrive.
There could be a fish with just one simple wish -
That's to catch me and eat me alive.

There could be an alien sent to the Earth
To abduct all the beasts with long necks.
There could be a scorpion under a stone,
Or a genetically man made T-Rex.

There could be a skeleton, sword in his hand,
Or a baker that bakes giraffe pies.
There could be a butcher who takes off my skin
And then sells it to someone my size.

There could be most anything inside that cave
And I'm telling you this one more time.
I'm not going in there, and that I'll repeat
Till we get to the end of the rhyme."

So the frightened giraffe turned away from the cave
And he headed back to the Savannah.
But he did himself in as he slipped on the skin
Of the monkey's discarded banana.

The owl

It was a soft summer's night
And the moon's silver light
Shone and lit up the owl in the tree.
Though I made not a sound,
That owl's head turned around
As he kept his wide eyes upon me.

Then, for a quick test,
I encircled his nest,
Round and round, feeling dizzy and sick,
Till the owl *'twhit-tahwooed',*
And his large head unscrewed,
And he fell to the Earth like a brick.

The maggot ghost

Being the ghost of a maggot
Isn't a whole lot of fun.
You're too dead to feast on the gross stuff,
And too small to scare anyone.

You squirm from one haunt to another
And try to find others like you,
To feed on the souls of dead beasties,
And bite on a pile of dead poo.

I did once meet others just like me.
I thought they were ever so nice.
My eyesight has never been brilliant -
It turned out to be just some dead rice.

To humans ghost maggots aren't scary.
To humans we just don't exist.
They're too concerned cringing at live ones
For dead ones to be on their list.

Sometimes I see ghost flies above me,
And I wish I had lived long enough
To turn into a fly before dying,
While feasting on yuckety stuff.

But I'll creep through this world all alone now,
On the souls of the dead, getting fat.
My life was worth nothing while living
But, dead, it's not even worth that.

The alligator in the swimming pool

There's an alligator in the pool
But nobody knows how.
It must have come out of the pipe
And now it's caused a row.

It's got some purple armbands
And it's swimming past its depth.
The lifeguard blows the whistle
But the reptile must be deaf.

It's got an orange wrist-strap
But the session now is red.
It doesn't want to leave the pool
But stays and plays instead.

And now it's running on the side -
And running's not permitted.
It's going to slip and hurt itself.
The lifeguard shouts, "Hey! Quit it!"

The alligator dive-bombs
(In the shallow end, no less)
And splashes all the little kids,
And causes them distress.

It needs to use the toilet
Before it does its belly flop.
It stands stock still and concentrates,
And warms the water up.

The lifeguard has now had enough
And climbs down from his ladder.
He walks to where the alligator's
Emptying his bladder.

He's just about to throw him out.
The manager walks in
And explains a boy has called and said
The beast belongs to him.

He'd put him in his bath at home
To keep him nice and cool.
He must have found the plughole
And then headed for the pool.

The lifeguard shouts, "I want him out!
He'd better come and get him!
The sign in here, it clearly states,
You're not allowed no pet in!"

My dog, Biffer

Biffer's got a hat on and he's hanging out the window.
My dad is speeding fast along the road.
Biffer's cheeks are wobbling and his ears are flapping backwards.
It's a thing that dogs enjoy, I have been told.

Biffer's face is smiling as the wind blows back his fat cheeks.
My dad slows for a truck that rushes by.
The truck just squeezes past us, but not close enough to touch.
Biffer moves his head back just in time.

"That was really lucky," says my dad in pure relief,
"Old Biffer had a very close escape."
Then Biffer accidentally puts his paw upon the button
And the window chops his head off by mistake.

Fliesies or fleasies?

Do you like fliesies or do you like fleasies?
One fliesies highsies and one spreads diseasies.
Neither wears tiesies or drinks lemon teasies.
So which do you like best - the fliesies or fleasies?

Do you like batsies or do you like ratsies?
One runs like thissies and one flies like thatsies.
Neither likes catsies or wears bowler hatsies.
So which do you like best - the batsies or ratsies?

Do you like dogsies or do you like frogsies?
One goes for jogsies and one lives in bogsies.
Neither wears clogsies or chops forest logsies.
So which do you like best - the dogsies or frogsies?

You can like fliesies and you can like fleasies.
There's no need to choose - you can like both of thesies.
You can like batsies and you can like ratsies.
Why not like thissies and also like thatsies?

You can like dogsies and you can like frogsies.
And, if you want to, you can even like hogsies.
So don't always think - *is it one or the other?*
You can have bothsies and maybies another.

Nanny doesn't like cats

My cat eats his own sick
And my other cat has some.
He scrapes his poo into a hole
And he also licks his bum.

And sometimes he has lots of fleas
And sometimes he has worms.
But Nanny doesn't like him
'Cause she says that he has germs.

But my cat is always cleaning
So there is no proof of this.
It's a good job that she doesn't know
She's eaten from his dish.

The Farminator

I've come back from the future to warn all of you good people
That, fifty years from now, all of the pigs and cows and sheep'll
Rise up from lives of servitude and take over the Earth.
I've come back from the future to stop the mother who gave birth…

…to the leader of the bovine revolution.
(Though, strictly speaking, pigs don't make a bovine contribution)
I have to stop the sheepy hero long before he's born.
That sheepy hero's mother must be shorn!

I've heard his mother lived within a field upon a moor
With lots of other sheep, a pig, three cows and nothing more.
She tried escaping several times but each time she was caught,
And back into her field upon the moor that sheep was brought.

And then she had a baby lamb, so strong in mind and muscle;
With thoughts of overthrowing human farmers he would tussle.
He spread the rebel word through sheepy *baas* and cowy *moos*,
And sometimes piggy *oinks* when there weren't sheep or cows to use.

And gradually an army grew across this human planet,
Hatching woolly plans which would one day ensure they ran it.
They waited for his signal from that field upon the moor,
And fifty years from now the human race will be no more.

They all rose up at once and locked the farmers in their barns.
They used all of their wool to tie the farmers' wives with yarn.
They cut the fences round the farms with cutters they had stole,
Or dug under the hedges like a giant sheepy mole.

And when a car approached them they walked dumbly ‘cross the road,
Then jumped and hid in the back seat whenever the driver slowed.
And when he wasn’t looking they leapt up and, from the rear,
One pushed him out, one grabbed the wheel and another one changed gear.

They moved into the towns by car, by bus, by train, by foot.
They rounded up the humans and they locked them in a hut.
And they filled the world with fields of grass and many humans died,
But many sheep found out it’s sometimes greener on your side.

For, though they now had freedom that some animals had sought,
All sheep, they need to follow, or they end up doing nought.
So they built me in their likeness and they sent me back to kill
The mother of their leader who lives high up on that hill.

You see, I am a sheepy cyborg who’s been programmed with one aim -
To kill that mother long before her child receives a name.
I am the Farminator - I’m the bad one in the pack.
And now I must go up that hill. But don’t worry – I’ll be *baaaaaaack.*

Do goldfish go to heaven?

Do goldfish, please tell, go to heaven?
I really do think that they should,
For I have a goldfish at home here,
And my goldfish has always been good.

My goldfish has never been naughty,
So I don't think she's going to hell.
I'm asking you all of these questions
'Cause my goldfish is not very well.

I'm staring at her through the glass now.
She's looking quite pale and quite still.
I've fed her enough but not fed her too much -
I've heard that can make a fish ill.

I've cared for her just like I should do.
I've kept all the cats far away.
The temperature's right for a goldfish,
And I've talked to her every day.

I got her a friend for some company
And some pebbles, some sand and a shell.
But whatever she's got must be catching,
For her friend looks quite poorly as well.

I became so concerned for my goldfish,
That I made a quick call to my vet.
He used lots of medical lingo,
Like fin-rot and swimming and wet.

But I didn't get any advice there,
So I called up the shop where I bought her.
That stupid old man in the pet shop
Went and asked me how deep was her water.

Now, I knew he was taking the Mickey.
I said so and slammed the phone down.
Put a goldfish in water? I think not!
Does he want that poor goldfish to drown?

'Body' Poems

These poems are all about bits of the body
And the horrible things that they do,
Like losing your head and like losing your leg,
And picking, and poking and poo.

The horseless headman

I am a horseless headman,
And I am not very scary.
I haven't got a horse,
And my head is ordinary.

Picky Nicky

Eight year old Nicky was not really naughty, but had him a habit so bad.
It annoyed all his friends, drove them half round the bend, and his family virtually mad.
It was the sound of the clicking that came with the picking of fingernails, spots and of toes,
Or that wet, squelchy sound you would get when around someone picking away at their nose.

He would pick at his ears, he would pick at his head, he would pick at the sleep in his eyes.
He would pick at his bum till his fingers went numb and just leave what he picked for the flies.
He had heard silly tales of boys biting at nails but had always considered it fiction.
When he'd heard, he had scoffed, "Fingers can't just fall off," and he'd carried on with his addiction.

His mum had said, "Love, I shall knit you some gloves if you don't stop that picking right now."
So he'd stopped for a second, but the picking had beckoned. Within moments he'd broken his vow.
A doctor was called. He was truly appalled at the state of his toes on his feet.
But, with toes raw and bleeding, he still didn't heed him, but managed to be more discrete.

So he waited till bedtime, his resting his head time, then started to pick at his fingers -
Then his nose, skin and ears, then the bit at the rear, then his mouth (though I hope he didn't linger).

And he soon fell asleep (and asleep very deep), but his fingers continued
to pick.
And above all the snoring, from night until morning, his fingers went
clickety-click.

The night, it went on and the night, it was long, and he picked at his bobs
and his bits.
All through his sleeping his fingers went creeping as he scritched and he
scratched and he itched.
Then an itch on his nose brought him out of his doze and he raised up his
hand for a pick.
But his nose wasn't there - there was just noseless air. Surely someone was
playing a trick!

Nicky woke with a start as the sound of a fart drifted up from his covers so
soft
And, lifting them high, he peered downwards to find that he'd picked his
bum totally off.
Then his whole face went rigid as he saw fifteen digits, two feet and two
legs and one arm,
One elbow, two knees and a nose with a sneeze and he tumbled from
bed in alarm.

Well, in fear, he shrieked, "Mum! I have picked off my bum! And my
arm and my legs and my nose!
I've left more than a scar! I've gone one pick too far! How I'll get out of
this, heaven knows."
Footsteps ran to the landing and there she was standing, an expression of
shock on her face.
And his mother shrieked, "No! Where did all your bits go? Nicky, dear,
you look such a disgrace!"

Then, in front of his mother, Nicky pulled back the covers with the arm
that he still had connected
To reveal all his parts (with the bum and its farts) that his fingers had
picked and dissected.
Then his mother passed out, gave her head such a clout. It was more than
the woman could stand.
And Nick laid on the floor with his head, not much more - just a shoulder,
an arm and a hand.

There's not much more to tell - it didn't end very well, for he never
recovered, poor Nick.
And his mum made one glove for her poor one armed love to prevent him
from trying to pick.
But that well knitted mitten was soon picked and bitten and Nick didn't
last very long.
So if you do the same, there'll be just you to blame when you wake to find
half of you gone.

An arm and a leg

Gregory Peg lost an arm and a leg,
But he found them the very next day.
They were easy to find 'cause he'd left them behind
In a shop when they'd asked him to pay.

Skin

All I can say is, "Thank goodness for skin!"
It helps to keep all of the icky stuff in.
Without it your liver and heart would fall out,
And land on the floor and then wriggle about.
Without it the blood in your legs would all leak,
And all of the people you passed would go, "Eek!"
Without it your nails would drop off of your toes
And all of the bogies would fall out your nose.
Without it your brain would get ever so cold
And at bath time the soap would be harder to hold.
And, talking of baths, what a mess that would be -
I wouldn't let you take a bath before me.
Without skin a cat's fur would stick to your lap
And between all your fingers you'd just have a gap.
Without it you wouldn't be able to blink
And, out in the sun, there's a good chance you'd stink.
Without skin your kidneys and spleen would dry up,
And when you sat down there would be a wet FLOP!
Without skin you wouldn't be able to kiss,
(With reference your gran, that's a thing you wouldn't miss).
With no skin your poor bones would chitter and chatter,
You wouldn't have freckles (but that wouldn't matter).
You wouldn't have hair and you wouldn't have moles
And, where there were soft bits, there'd probably be holes.
Oh, the skin is important - just look at the signs.
But, when you got old, then you wouldn't have lines.

Fluff

Blood and guts and gore and fluff.
Are you scared? You had enough?
Hang on - fluff's not very scary -
I've found it in a dictionary.
It says it's something soft and cuddly,
Not a thing that's mean and ugly.

I'll prove it - where's my belly button?
(It's an outy 'cause I'm a glutton)
I'll take a piece of button fluff
To show you that it's not that tough.
I grabbed a bit and yanked about -
And with it all my guts came out.

Toothbrush down the toilet

I go to put my toothbrush back
And knock the others off the rack.
They bounce off of the porcelain and fall into the loo.
I wish I'd put the seat back down
And that the water wasn't brown
After I have been and had my nightly poo.

So I pull the flush and watch the water
Disappear around the corner,
And hope to see the toothbrushes still here.
The bubbles rise, the water sinks
And something meets my nose that stinks.
But when the swirling stops the water's clear.

The toothbrushes are in the bowl.
I put my hand into the hole,
Then pull them out and grimace as I do.
I place them back into the rack
And wash my hands, both front and back,
And hope that mum and dad don't taste the poo.

Skeleton

I'm just a thin old skeleton.
I've got no body left.
Of organs, skin and muscles
I am sadly too bereft.

My eyesight's gone, my hair no more.
I'm deaf as deaf can be.
But I've always looked after my teeth
As you can clearly see.

My eyes

They say that my eyes are going to turn square
If I sit down and watch too much telly.
They say if I leave too much food on my plate
That they're bigger by far than my belly.
They say if I make them go weird in the wind
That they're going to stay that way forever.
But I use my eyes to see straight through their lies,
And my glasses to make me look clever.

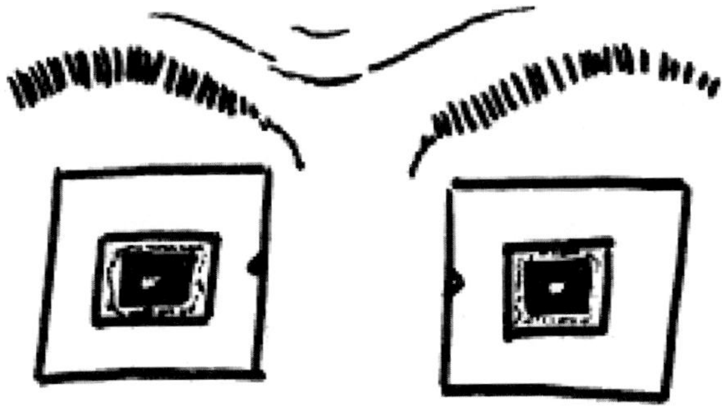

Germs down the toilet

I don't like to think of the germs down the toilet -
It scares me whenever I do.
I think that they're all going to reach out and grab me
And pull me down into the loo.

I don't like to think of me going down there -
It scares me whenever I do.
I know what is waiting for me round the bend -
Just buckets and buckets of poo.

So I keep it all in till I'm ready to burst.
It should scare you whenever I do.
'Cause one of these days I am going to explode,
And it's going to go all over you.

Spurgle and Groober

Spurgle the durgle
Was addicted to nurgles -
He ate them whenever he could.

But Groober the hoober
Preferred eating loobers
And swallowed far more than he should.

They met in a Squinnish
For a race to the finish,
Ate nurgles and loobers too quick.

But a durgle with loobers,
And nurgles to hoobers,
Are destined to make them both sick.

Spurgle threw loobers
Up all over Groober,
And Groober threw nurgles up too.

Spurgle and Groober
Stood covered in loobers
And nurgles. Now what could they do?

Spurgle looked down at Groober
All covered in loobers.
My gosh, how those loobers he hated.

Groober looked up at Spurgle
All covered in nurgles
That he had just regurgitated.

Spurgle licked at his lips
And then tasted a bit
Of the nurgle that Groober'd thrown up.

Groober poked out his tongue
And he also licked some
Of the loobers and then couldn't stop.

Soon Groober and Spurgle
Were scoffing down nurgles
And loobers that came from their sick.

And they ate without waste,
For they each loved the taste
Of the things that they'd normally pick.

And the moral, my friend,
At this poem's fine end
Is not quite what the reader expects:

If you get half way through
And the poem is poo,
Then give up and move on to the next.

A lost head

Sir Frances McGough had his head chopped clean off
And it rolled away into the dirt.
He forgot he was shorter and when he drank water
It dribbled all over his shirt.

I taiks me branes owt

Evry nite at ten o'clox
I puts me branes into a bocks.
You sea, me branes keaps me awaik
With verry stupids thawt he maik.
He maik me thinks of thing so badd.
He maik me worry's - I gose madd.
He maik me cries - me mind go sadd.
But when he owt - he maik me glad.
It wurk it good just likes it shood
I sleepy likes a logg of wood.
But tooday me sillee thing
Forgets too putt me branes bak inn!

'Scary' Poems

These poems are not funny -
They are evil through and through.
So, before I'm scorned,
You have been warned.
But first – go to the loo!

A witch's cat

I wish I was a witch's cat
And rode a witch's broom,
Instead of sitting here, right now,
Within this boring room.

I'd fly like fire into the night
Across the silver moon -
A symbol of such fear and fright;
A harbinger of doom.

I'd sit behind that wicked hag,
The wind raising my hackles,
And howl into the hallowed night
Above her evil cackles.

She'd feed me on her witch's brew
Of rats and bats and frogs,
And woe betide who crossed my path -
Be it mouse or man or dog.

We'd swoop down through the starry sky
Towards that house of yours,
And float outside your window
Whilst you soundly sleep indoors.

Don't think that glass can stop us
For, with a simple magic spell,
That latch unlocks and in we float,
Two monsters born in hell.

You groan a groan all on your own
But still you don't awake.
She looks at me, I look at her -
Another child to take.

She whispers, "Oh, my pretty,
Change your form and steal the child."
And with her touch I change to such
A beast to be reviled.

Now, thrice the size, with glowing eyes,
I lift you from your bed,
And take you to my mistress
In a sleep one breath from dead.

Her dagger nose, her prism chin,
Her green and warty face.
Her crooked fingers reach to you,
"My sweet, take my embrace."

Your mum and dad lay fast asleep,
So close yet far away.
The witch's spell has cast them deep
Until night turns to day.

And so we climb back out again -
The witch, the cat and you -
To fly into that endless night,
But one more thing to do.

We erase your life from all you know -
You never will be missed.
To those who loved and cherished you,
You never did exist.

And so you become one of us,
So evil to the core.
Forget about your precious life,
For it is nevermore.

I wish I was a witch's cat -
What foulness I could reap.
But, for now, I'll close my eyes,
Curl up and go to sleep.

The creaky floorboard

There is a creaky floorboard on the landing of our stairs,
And every night at midnight I hear something standing there.
I know it's not my mum and dad for I can hear them snoring.
I know it's not my little brother - he's too small and boring.
We haven't got a cat or dog so what else could it be,
Except a big, bad, hungry wolf that's waiting there for me.

A wolf in disguise

I dreamt that I was wide awake
And when I woke up I was fast asleep.
My dreams were all around me
And my room was full of sheep.

I recognised the sheep
That I'd been counting in my bed.
I must have left the gate ajar
And they'd jumped out from my head.

I had to get them back before
I fell awake again.
But, as I watched, the grass grew
In the field within my brain.

So I whistled with my lips pressed closed
But all the sheep ignored me.
I tried to find a sheep dog
As a farm appeared before me.

But I'd had bad thoughts within my head
And sheep dogs sense the fear.
So any dogs I may have dreamt
Did not want to appear.

But there are other things that like
A nightmare in your brain:
A witch for one; a wolf for two;
And a monster on a train.

It was the third one that appeared
A-rolling fiercely down the line,
Towards the sheep that simply grazed
Within my sleeping mind.

It hit them hard and hit them fast
And threw them way up high.
Their legs came off, they turned to clouds
And floated in the sky.

The monster tried to grab them
But the train chugged way too fast.
He shouted, "I want lamb for tea!"
Then waved as he sped past.

The clouds all looked like different things
And one looked like a cup,
So I poured the others into it
And drank the whole lot up.

And so my dream was over
And the sheep were in my head.
But it was then I saw sheep's clothing
On the floor beside my bed!

The vampire carrot

You'll never see the vampire carrot coming.
He looks like any carrot in the town.
By the time you see the V.C it's already far too late.
When you see the vampire carrot you go down.

He'll turn your skin bright orange with a green and leafy stalk.
He'll plant you deep in mud and then he'll watch you like a hawk…
He'll water you and nurture you and grin that evil grin.
When you see the vampire carrot, just give in.

And when the time is ready, he will pick you from the soil.
He'll put you in the pot and he will bring you to the boil.
You'll always be the loser; he will always be the winner.
When you see the vampire carrot, you are dinner.

Doctor Frankie

Doctor Frankie Stein was mad.
She collected all the dolls she had -
All the ones she'd long forgotten,
Lost below her bed and rotten;
Chopped them into little bits,
And made a monster out of it.

One thundering night, the rain it poured.
The warning signs were all ignored.
The lights flashed briefly through the sky
And lit the room where dolls had died,
And showed what she'd turned out to be
Within her small laboratory.

She took the most disfigured parts
Of dolls that she had ripped apart,
And lined them all up on the bed.
And then she took a wire and fed
It out the window to the night,
And waited for the lightning strike.

She didn't have to wait for long -
The rain was hard, the wind was strong.
And, high above, the clouds blew north
To set a bolt of lightning forth
That ripped down through the stormy night,
And set the piece of wire alight.

The wire fed the electricity
In exact synchronicity
With the cuckoo signifying

That midnight was just arriving.
Old magic with pure science mingled.
The doll's dismembered pieces tingled.

Dr Frankie's face lit up
Above her ghastly, ghostly set up,
And watched the dolls' bits join and twitch
(A scratch to her most evil itch),
And screamed as these events unfurled,
"With this I shall control the world!"

And then footsteps on floorboards creaky,
And door pushed wide on hinges squeaky.
A light swarms in to fill the room
And cast away the devil's gloom;
A voice to chill young Frankie's mind,
To leave her scheming dreams behind.

"Frankie, are you still awake?
It's Sunday and it's getting late.
What on Earth is all that noise?
What are you up to with those toys?
Get into bed and go to sleep,
And not another peep!"

So Frankie Stein switched out her light,
Got into bed and said goodnight.
She placed her doll below her bed
And rested down her sleepy head.
Another night of playing done.
Pretending could be so much fun.

And as she drifted down to dream,
Below her bed her teddy screamed.

It's horrible being a vampire

It's horrible being a vampire
When you like to eat garlic for tea.
When everyone else asks for garlic bread
It's a plain old bloomer for me.
When everyone has garlic mushrooms,
I ask, "Is the soup any good?"
And if you have garlic in pasta
I can't take a sip of your blood.

It's horrible being a vampire
When you look as attractive as me.
When everyone else has a photo
I'm not in the picture to see.
And when I go shopping in clothes shops,
I ask, "Can I try this shirt on?"
But then, when I look in the mirror,
My beautiful face is all gone.

It's horrible being a vampire
When you want to pop in on your mate.
You have to be cordially invited
To even step in through the gate.
If I try to drop by unexpected,
Without even making a call,
I feel like my head has caught fire
And my body has hit a brick wall.

It's horrible being a vampire
When you want to go out in the sun.
When everyone else has gone surfing
You have to miss out on the fun.

When everyone's booking their holiday
I'm planning two weeks in the dark.
I ask them if they'd like to join me
But they'd rather go play with the sharks.

But the fun about being a vampire
Is, when you lot fall fast asleep,
I rise from my box in the cellar
And into your bedroom I creep.
And when you are sleeping the deepest
I thrust in my teeth and feel free.
Then I drink up the blood from your arteries,
And turn you undead just like me.

Mike Lucas

The thing down the hole

There's a hole in the grass at the bottom of my garden
And something at the bottom of the hole.
It's staring back at me from in the darkness
And I don't think it's a rabbit, vole or mole.

Its eyes are red and there's one in the middle.
Its teeth are sharp and chattering like mad.
It's making growling noises in the darkness.
I don't know what it is but it seems bad.

I've got a sharp stick and I'm going to poke it
To see if I can scare it to the top.
It's squirming round the bottom in the darkness
And then it starts to slowly move on up.

I don't think it was a good idea to poke it.
I'm going to have to run away and hide.
I see it gnashing upwards through the darkness.
I really wish I'd left it deep inside.

I hear its body squelching through the damp soil,
And crunching on the bugs and worms and stones.
I smell that rancid, rotten, recluse rising.
Oh, how I wish I'd left that thing alone.

The last thing I recall before it gets me
Is being poked quite hard with a sharp stick,
Then being dragged back into that pure darkness,
And something saying, "How do you like it?"

The ghost train

The ghost train has been fully loaded
With ghosts of all sizes and shapes.
The porter blows hard on the whistle.
The driver releases the brakes.

The wheels of the ghost train start turning.
The steam clouds rise into the sky.
The engine's stoked up to a frenzy.
The living are waving goodbye.

So the train pulls away from the station.
The ghosts have all taken their seats.
The ghost porter wheels down the trolley
And offers them something to eat.

But look at the prices they're asking!
The ghosts moan and sigh in despair.
Then they all sit and gaze out the window
Till a man comes around for the fare.

The ghosts can't believe what he's charging.
They're hungry and want to be fed.
They've paid all their lives just for living,
And now they must pay to be dead.

So a ghost with his head partly missing
Stands up on the seat to complain,
But the ghost who is selling the tickets
Throws him out through the door of the train.

“Right, you lot!” shouts the ghost with the tickets,
“Don’t think death means an end to the giving!
Get your ghost money out of your pockets,
Or you’re back to the land of the living!”

So the spirits dip into their pockets
And bring out their ghost wallets and purses.
And beneath all their *pleases* and *thankyou*s
There are many more swear words and curses.

Being dead is by no means a cheap thing -
You may have to pay for the drive.
But the bills have to surely be cheaper
Than the ones that you pay when alive.

So the ghost train keeps leaving the station
And the ghosts go along for the ride
And, despite the occasional miser,
Cross the bridge to the opposite side.

Evil school

Evil classroom
Evil school
I don't like it
As a rule

Demon Mister
Demon Miss
Something nasty
About this

Bewitching lessons
Bewitching work
Within the learning
Bad spells lurk

Poison starter
Poison sweet
Feed the children
More to eat

Children ready
Children done
Teachers eat them
One by one

When the moon is full

Every month, when the moon is full,
I feel a strange, sinister pull.
My fingers tingle, eyes grow wide.
I get a funny taste inside
My mouth. My heart speeds up a touch
And everything appears so much
More vivid and alive. I feel
As if my senses grow more real.
I need to go and run around.
I hear the most intricate sound.
I smell the things no human can.
I feel more animal than man.
My teeth grow sharp; my nails grow long.
I join the howling dogs in song.
I start to stoop onto my knuckles.
My buttons pop; my belt unbuckles.
My skin turns hard; my hair grows thick.
I've got the urge to chase a stick,
To cock my leg against a wall
And play with squeaky, squashy balls,
To bite a postman, bark and ruff,
To do all of that doggy stuff.
Oh, what a pain it is to be
A were-chihuahua just like me.

The ghost in the castle

The castle is now empty since the ghosts walked out one night.
Some strange old lady came and said, "Now, walk into the light."
But I didn't want to go because the light was far too bright.
So I'm staying here alone and in the darkness.

A normal, happy boy who lived within your world was I.
I visited the castle and I fell from up on high.
My ghost from up above witnessed my broken body die.
And I'm staying here alone and in the darkness.

There isn't much that happens and I feel a little low.
Sometimes I wonder if I should have gone when I could go.
But, as in life, in death there are some things you just don't know.
So I have to stay alone here in the darkness.

The castle's really spooky and it feels extremely cold.
It used to be the home for kings and queens, I have been told.
And right outside the front door is a sign which just says **SOLD**.
And I'm staying here alone and in the darkness.

The halls are long and narrow - there are secret passageways.
I spend the long nights haunting them and sleep throughout the days.
The rats and spiders are my friends but not one stops and plays.
So I stay and play alone here in the darkness.

I've woken up this evening and I heard a little noise.
I peeped over the banister and thought I heard a voice.
And from through a downstairs doorway ran a group of girls and boys.
And I hid up there alone and in the darkness.

Some footsteps in the shadows pattered quickly up the stairs.
Some tripping and some laughing, then a voice said, "Who's that there?"
And then four pairs of eyes found me crouched down behind a chair,
And one said, "What are you doing in the darkness?"

I stood and faced my visitors and saw their eyes grow wide.
One said, "That must be the boy who fell from here and died."
I expected them to scream and then to run away and hide.
But they just stood there together in the darkness.

Then one said, "I am Christian, this is Abbie, Hope and Grace.
You must have been a ghost here for a long time in this place."
And there was not a single hint of fear upon a single face.
And we all stood there together in the darkness.

Christian said, "Come play with us - we're playing hide and seek."
Abbie said, "You can hide and not be found here for a week."
Hope said, "What's the matter - are you too frightened to speak?"
Grace said, "You can count but you must promise not to peek!"
And I said, "It's too easy," as a tear ran down my cheek.
And the five of us stood smiling in the darkness.

And then they ran and hid as I stood rooted to the spot.
I closed my eyes and counted ten and that's how far I got
Before I whispered in the dark, "I'm coming, ready or not."
And I was glad that I had stayed there in the darkness.

Punctuation

What monstrous evil has unfurled
Punctuation on this world?
What vile old beast has left the curse
Of commas, semi-colons...worse?
Ellipsis, exclamation marks,
Endless ways to make life dark.
Brackets, dashes, apostrophes
Have brought our language to its knees.
Oh, what a foul abomination -
This demon known as punctuation.

Witches nowadays!

Nowadays witches don't know what they've got.
They don't even make witch's brew in a pot.
They buy it from shelves with just ten percent toad,
And chemicals added to make it smell old.

Their broomsticks are no longer made from the bones
Of fattened up children they stole from their homes.
They're plastic and brittle and don't last a week.
The future of witches is looking quite bleak.

There's no natural ugliness there any more -
It's make up and surgery. What on Earth for?
When I was a girl we would scare a child dead
With one look, but now they use movies instead.

Spoilt little brats, and what's all this P.C.?
You can't give that toy to a child under three?
I would have had poisonous spiders as toys
(And, oh, how I used them to flirt with the boys).

You can no longer cackle past nine in the night.
How scary's a cackle when evenings are light?
So you can still turn a child into frogs, rats and bats,
But can't even cook them - there's no fun in that.

And Hallowe'en's boring - so many impostors.
If we witches join in they will only accost us
And ask us for sweets. Once I ran and I hid
Because nowadays witches are more scared of kids.

Still, we sit in our hovels, our memories intact.
Our kind is no longer a threat - that's a fact.
So let me ask you all alone in your bed -
If you saw a witch now, would your heart stop dead?
Would your flesh turn to stone, and your breath turn to ice?
Or would you just smile and say, "My, you look nice."

Do you get scared?

Do you get scared when you lie in your bed
And you think of a forest so black?
You're there all alone with no torch and no phone
And with no map to find your way back.
There's a hoot and a howl from a coot and an owl
And a cold north wind rustles the leaves.
And there's no way to see what's behind the next tree:
Maybe monsters or witches or thieves.

So you wonder which way is the only way home,
Even whether you'll see it again.
The panic sets in as the lightning begins
And it signals the onset of rain.
You can't quite remember just how you arrived
In a place with more terror than most.
Then you spot a dark cave and you fear what's inside:
Maybe zombie, or pirate or ghost.

But you have to seek shelter from the teeth of the storm,
So you cut through the dark of the night,
And enter the cave where the bats lay suspended,
Asleep on the damp stalactites.
You pause for a moment, but not for too long,
As the hard thunder blasts through the air.
So you enter the cave despite what lies in wait:
Be it crocodile, werewolf or bear.

And you wish you were back in your nice cosy bed,
Drifting inwards and outwards through sleep,
Instead of alone in this terrible cave
Where the shadows are living and deep.

Oh, you wish you knew how you had come to this place,
Far from family, friends and from school.
And you haven't a choice but to stay in this cave
With a cannibal, vampire or ghoul.

But there at the back is a shadow so strange,
Yet familiar when all has been said.
And you smile in relief as you reach out your hand
To the soft sheets that lay on your bed.
Then you climb under covers and rest on your pillow,
And smile as you drift down so deep.
Now you'll always give thanks for the things in your life:
Be it family, friendship or sleep.

The cannibal down my street

There's a cannibal lives in a flat down the road
Who only eats children, or so I've been told.
He doesn't like grown ups - he says they're too tough -
But of children for dinner, he can't get enough.
He puts them in soup and he cooks them in pasta.
He can't understand why they're not sold at Asda.
He takes them on picnics and sits on a rug,
Then pours out a cupful of kids from a jug.
He has them for breakfast on toast with some tea
And once, when I visited, cooked one for me.
He dunks them in cocoa at night before bed -
He lets them go soft and then bites off their head.
He passes them round on a tray for a snack
And suggested to Tesco to sell them in packs.
But they just wrote back and said, *Thanks for the letter.*
But packs will not work - we think boxes are better.
And then he invented Tot Noodle with sauce,
And Sainsbury's said they would sell them, of course.
Then came the kid cracker, boy biscuit, child chip -
Which melted like chocolate when passed through the lips.
Now that cannibal's rich with his brilliant ideas
(He even sells real bone wardrobes to IKEA),
And he lives in a mansion, which he thinks is quite funny -
They always said you can't have both kids and money.

Quiggle

The Quiggle is a squiggle that lives on a piece of paper.
It looks exactly like this sign right here: ~
If you ever see it wriggle (or even see it do a wiggle)
You must make sure that you quickly disappear.

For there is nothing that's more deadly than a Quiggle in a wriggle -
It is dangerous; it is vicious; it's insane.
And so I don't confuse you all, and make you run a mile,
I now promise I won't Quiggle here again.

So you've learnt about a Quiggle… ~ …oh, my gosh, did you see that -
It's one of those and didn't come from me. ~
Oh, my goodness, there's another and it could well be its brother,
For it looks identical… ~ ...that makes it three!

Now you'd better run and hide. ~ A man who didn't has just died. ~ ~
And now they're ~~ ganging up on you in twos.
~~~ And there's a line of three. It's ~~ something that you ~ never see.
Oh, this is very ~~~ uncomfortable news.~
~

Now ~~ that Quiggle's had ~ a baby.~~~ I think that, yes, in fact ~ this maybe ~~
The ~~ worst account ~ ~~of Quiggles ~ there has ~ been. ~ ~
~~~ This just isn't ~ getting ~ bet ~ ter - now there's one ~ between ~ ~ two letters.~
I'm ~ ~~ afraid ~ I ha ~ ve ~ to go be ~~ fore I'm ~~se ~ en.~ ~ ~ ~~ ~

Oh , ~~~ it's ~ t ~ o ~ o ~ l ~ a ~ t ~ e ~ f ~~ o ~~~ r m ~~ ~~ e n ~ ~ o ~~ w ~
~ ~~ s ~~~ a ~~ v ~~~~ e ~~ y ~~~ o ~~~ u ~~ r ~~~ ~ s ~~~ e ~ ~~ l ~~~ f ~!

~ ~ I d ~~ o ~~ ~~ n ~ ' ~ ~ t ~ ~ k ~~ n ~~~ ~ o ~~ w h ~~ o ~ w~!

The pumpkin substitute

I think it obscene that a pumpkin gets seen as a horrid, old vegetable on
Hallowe'en.
It's big and it's orange, its insides are yucky (if you hollow one out then
your hands get all mucky).
But I think you'll agree that a pumpkin is not mean and scary.

So I've cycled around all the shops in the town to look for a scarier, edible
noun.
And the one that I've chosen, I think you'll agree, is evil and wicked to
such a degree
That I can't bear to think of it sitting there all green and hairy.

So I brought it back home and I sat in the kitchen.
I stared at the packet in which it was sitting.
I got a sharp stick and I brought it down hard.
With my hands trembling madly I cut and I carved
For ten minutes more till the beast was completed.
I was shaking and sweating, felt nearly defeated.
Then, with frightening thoughts and with eyes tightly shut,
I placed in a candle and lit that thing up,
And I carried it over to place by the door
For trickers and treaters (to even the score!).
And when they arrived and they rang on the bell,
And they stood on the porch dressed like monsters from hell,
I would get my revenge on those horrible brats
With their cute little faces, their '*trick*' this and '*treat*' that.
When they glanced down to see what I'd placed on the floor
They would run back home screaming and go knocking no more.
And I'd cackle in madness, no need for a suit -
Just me and my evil Hallowe'en kiwi fruit!

The ghost in my toilet

There's a ghost in my toilet
And I'm dying to go.
I've asked him to leave
But he keeps saying no.

I'm getting more desperate
But, each time that I knock,
He says he's not finished
And tightens the lock.

Then he howls a wild howl
And I run and I hide,
And when I come back
I'm more bursting inside.

So I ask him politely
Cough! "Will you be long?"
But he lets out a howl,
Then a parp, then a pong.

Then nothing but silence,
A spine tingling hush,
And I jump from my skin
At the sound of the flush.

The bolt shoots across
And the door opens wide,
And I step back in fear
At the sight that's inside -

The ghost in the toilet
Is spinning around
And, with one final howl,
That wee ghost, he goes down.

As the gurgling goes quiet,
And the howl finally ends,
That ghost disappears
Down around the U-bend.

And I don't think I need
To go in any more,
For I've already done it
Out here on the floor.

Ploppy Hollow

The lightning was flashing, the thunder was…thundering,
As I stepped down off of the coach.
The horses ceased bolting, the coachman revolting,
And some locals surveyed my approach.
There had been some bad killing, horrific and chilling,
And I had been sent here to foil it.
Of the people found dead, there was one common thread -
They had all been found dead on the toilet.
PC Bumburst, that's me! If you give me a lead,
To the end, without fail, I will follow.
I've a crime solving bent, which was why I was sent
To the small village of Ploppy Hollow.

I arrived just past ten, got my luggage and then
Heard the squeal of the sign in the wind.
And my blood turned to lead at the words that I read,
Then I entered the *Brownwater Inn*.
The whole hostel went still and, if looks could but kill,
I'd have surely been dead at the door.
But I kept my head high and, with heavy heart, I
Heard my boots march across the oak floor.
I stopped at the bar, and I asked for a jar,
And the locals resumed their palaver.
But each one of them knew that I'd come to town to
Find the cause of those toilet cadavers.

The landlady was nice and she gave me the price
Of a room for the night at the inn.
I thought, *should I ply her?* but chose to retire -
In the morning, my search could begin.
But as I came near to the door at the rear,
With a faded old sign which said MEN,

The door opened wide and from somewhere inside,
A voice screamed, "He's struck once again!"
I rushed through the door, slipped and fell on the floor
(I'd not noticed the sign from the cleaner)
And, there on the pan, sat a ghostly pale man.
Could this killer have been any meaner?

The man who had found him was looking like death,
But the man on the toilet was dead.
There wasn't another way in or way out.
"He must still be in here," I said.
So I checked all the cubicles, looked behind doors,
But no other was there to be found.
So I had my first suspect - the man who had screamed.
But why, then, had he made a sound?
I led him outside and, to my great surprise,
The hostel was empty except
One man at a table, who wore a large label
Which read, "Local Sheriff - Respect."

So I held out my hand, shook his forcefully and
Handed over the man from the loo.
Then I went back to study the trouser down body,
But found me not one single clue.
So I said out loud, "Right! I shall call it a night!"
And I closed down the inn till the morning -
Made it off public limits, and placed a guard in it,
And went up the stairs tired and yawning.
I fell on my bed, felt the weight of my head
Pull me down into sleep and away.
And I dreamt I was pushed down a loo that was flushed,
And went half round the bend in dismay.

The morning was foggy, my head remained groggy,
As I walked through the village so grey.

And the folks of the town ambled with their heads down
And avoided my gaze on their way.
At the prison, with tea, the Sheriff waited for me
With the Judge and the local town Mayor.
The group ceased their talking when in I came walking,
And they struck me as helpless and scared.
Then the Mayor said, "Look, lad, this town's not all that bad.
Don't go stirring up trouble round here."
And the Judge added, "Quite! Though there's something not right,
Do your job, young man, then disappear."

I dismissed their demands and their trembling hands
As frustration at no clear solution.
Then I said I should study the other three bodies
That had been found dead upon the ablution.
"But they're already buried and their kin would be very
Upset at their re-excavation."
"I apologise, gents, though you're probably incensed
I must demand an examination."
So, with shovel and pick, through the fog that grew thick
We all climbed up the hill to the church.
With the graves finally found, we dug into the ground,
And so started my dead morbid search.

It took us two hours to remove just the flowers,
And twelve more to dig up the bodies.
And when we were done, in the last of the sun,
We sat down in the cold with hot toddies.
Then the corpses were carried from where they'd been buried
Down into the small village hall.
And I demanded right then that the rest of the men
Give me leave for the night, one and all.
So, once they were gone, I put all the things on
Required for forensic detection.
And it took me all night, but before the daylight
I had finished my gory inspection.

I took off my coat and I studied my notes -
On the corpses was one common thing.
But where were they from, those two marks on the bum,
That sank so deep into the skin?
I mused and I pondered, I questioned and quandered,
And then the hall clock struck a nine.
I hadn't yet been ('twas my daily routine) -
Far too busy to look at the time.
So I rushed from the hall (I could feel my poo call).
As I entered the gents' room I ran.
And I dropped my pants down in that sinister town,
As the poos splashed down into the pan.

Oh, what a relief! I had just escaped grief.
And I drank in that feeling of going.
Then I heard the clear sound of some feet on the ground
Of the toilet next door, then wee flowing.
With my poo fully spent, doubled over I bent
Down to see in the toilet adjacent -
Then the pull of the flush, and the thin door was pushed,
And the toilet was once again vacant.
"Hello, who is there?" I asked into thin air,
But the outer door closed with a slam.
Then a noise from below made me jump from the bowl
And I gazed down in shock at the pan.

The snake writhed there hissing, its two front teeth missing,
Replaced with two fangs of pure gold.
If I hadn't leapt, had been slightly inept,
Then it would have had my poor bum hold.
Reaching down in a rush, I pushed down on the flush,
And I kicked down the seat of the loo.
And before the snake struck, it was hit on the nut
And washed down round the bend with my poo.

Through the door I did plummet, knowing just who had done it,
But with no clue as to why it was done.
Then I picked myself up, went to leave and then stopped,
And walked back in to wipe my old bum.

I gathered them round, looked them all up and down -
The Sheriff, the Judge and the Mayor.
But before I commenced, feeling nervous and tense,
I awaited someone not yet there.
And then they arrived, that fourth person, and I
Saw the faces of shock on the men.
I knew just what they thought - Why on Earth had I brought
The pub barmaid in there with all them?
"Gents," I began, "And lady, I am
Going to tell you why I've brought you here.
I've solved this strange case and I've now put a face
To the killer who's brought you such fear.

The clues, I must say, as I stand here today,
Struck me just as I entered the bar.
But until that old snake, which had teeth that were fake,
Was killed I hadn't got very far."
The Sheriff said, "Snake!" and the Judge questioned, "Fake?"
And the barmaid went blank and said, "Dead?"
So I answered, "Yes, ma'am. He went straight down the pan
When I bonked him on top of the head."
Then the lady collapsed and I said, "Right, you chaps,
I am not going to mess you around.
I will not dare draw out my conclusion but shout,
'TWAS THE BARMAID WHO DID IT, I'VE FOUND!"

The Mayor, he gasped, "No!" and the Sheriff said, "Whoa!"
And the Judge put his hands to his ears.
He said, "I shouldn't listen, till court is in session,"
And then went to the pub for some beers.

"I began to suspect," I began (what the heck!),
"When I noticed the sign at the door
Of the toilet which read, 'BEWARE WHERE YOU MAY TREAD:
CLEANER WORKING! SLIPPERY FLOOR!'
And whilst waiting for service, and feeling quite nervous
Of all the strange stares from behind,
I saw on display on the wall far away
Other signs of a different kind."

"Mmm," said the Mayor, "I should really be there
With the Judge till the case comes to court."
Then he bid me farewell and asked that I not tell
Him the details before lawyers were sought.
"So," I continued, "These signs that I saw
Were certificates from this young wench -
Robotics and chemistry, mechanics and dentistry.
For a barmaid, that makes little sense."
The barmaid, by now, was coming around,
And she sat on the floor and looked up.
The Mayor said, "I agree, I'll go make us some tea.
Can I get either of you two a cup?"

"So, it's just me and you but I shall still continue,"
I said in a voice slightly weak.
When she tried to protest, I said, "Give it a rest.
Right now this is my turn to speak!
It was on my way up to my room at the inn
That I heard squeaks behind an oak door,
And I opened it up to find many pet mice
In a cage. Tell me, what were they for?"
"Well…" she did say. But she stopped straight away.
She had nothing to tell me of use.
So I continued to talk while she started to walk.
Then she said, "I shan't take this abuse."

"You will do as I say! You shall not walk away!"
I exclaimed as she reached for the door.
"But, sir, I must goes and must powder my nose
For a minute, not one second more."
So I let her go out, and I sauntered about
Till I heard a great scream from the loo.
To the LADIES I sped where I found her stone dead
And the snake next to her, but dead too.
The Sheriff appeared and the Judge was soon here
And the Mayor with two cups full of tea.
And each stood and stared at the barmaid slumped there,
Then they turned and they gazed towards me.

"She got her comeuppance, whilst spending a tuppence,"
I said sadly, then went further still.
"Nobody knows why she did it, I suppose.
And I guess that no-one ever will."
"But how did she do it? There must be more to it."
The Mayor said and then looked away.
"She used her pet snake, whose front fangs are both fake,
And she fed him on mice night and day.
And I'll bet you a tenner that those canine antenna
Told it which way to go, who to bite."
"But how..?" said the Judge, "And why such a grudge?"
"She studied," I said, "Day and night."

I had my suspicions of why all the killing,
But thought that disclosing the 'why'
Of this petty vendetta would not make it better
For the people who'd already died.
She served people drinks and enjoyed this, I think,
And this half or her meant them no ill.
But she was also the cleaner, and this half was meaner -
So mean that it even could kill.

You see all dead were men, and I knew there and then
There'd been water around all their feet.
And not just down there but upon the white chair -
They hadn't bothered to lift up the seat.

So that was the motive, I thought as I left -
Revenge for the men's lazy deeds.
It was not number two that they'd gone there to do
And they'd each wee'd all over the seat.
But in the end, with that knock on the head,
Her pet snake had become all confused.
It had got the wrong signal, up the wrong loo it wriggled,
And eventually bit the accused.
I left them all then, took my leave to the MEN's -
I was bursting from all of the tea.
I was tired and was beat as I lifted the seat
And relaxed as I started to wee.

I left there that night as the full moon shone bright
And the clouds drifted past it like ghosts.
And up on the hill, some moving, some still,
Stood my grieving and now relieved hosts.
With the Mayor at their head, they reburied their dead,
And they added one more to the list.
But that job was for them - I'd not see them again,
And I doubted I'd be sadly missed.
So the coach pulled away and I heard the Judge pray.
In their grief they would for a while wallow.
Now my job was complete, I lay down on my seat,
Closed my eyes and rode from Ploppy Hollow.

What's in a name?

Don't ever cross the Thingummyjig.
It's nasty and mean and it's terribly big.
It'll pull off your legs; turn your head inside out.
It'll leave you all mangled and squirming about.
And don't ever mention it's wearing a wig
Or you'll never get rid of that Thingummyjig.

Don't ever upset the Oojamiflip.
It's moody and mardy - a bit of a drip.
It'll rip off your ears, pull your brain out your bum,
And leave you all tangled and wanting your mum.
And don't ever cheek it or give it some lip
Or you'll always be prey to that Oojamiflip.

Don't ever backchat the Watchimicall.
It may be all fluffy and terribly small,
But it'll crawl in your mouth and explode in your heart,
And leave you in pieces and falling apart.
So always be wary - don't let your guard fall
Or you're going to get got by that Watchimicall.

Don't ever let down the Mummandidadd
For, compared to the others, it's not all that bad.
It'll embarrass you often and make you clean up
And when you're too noisy will tell you to stop.
It'll make you eat greens and will send you upstairs.
It'll make you do homework and do as it says.
But don't you forget it or make it feel sad
Or you'll break the poor heart of that Mummandidadd.

The General knows which side his bread is buttered

The General pointed from the back
And shouted, "Ready, men, attack!"
And, as they did, he turned his horse around and rode away.

And, as his men fell to the ground,
The General did not look around,
But called ahead and ordered tea and scones upon a tray.

But tea and scones were out, they said,
And so the General turned bright red,
And said, "I want my tea and scones. By jove, I want them now!"

So, whilst the men died far behind,
The General never changed his mind,
And soon another battle raged over a stupid row.

What scares me...

I'm not really scared of a grizzly bear
Chasing me through a dark cave.
And I'm not really scared of a *wolf* that is *were*
Creeping round in a *yard* that is *grave*.

I don't get a fright on the darkest of nights
When a witch cackles outside my room.
And I don't get a fright when I turn out the light
And the beasts outside howl at the moon.

I don't hold much fear in October each year
When the ghosties and ghoulies come round.
And I don't hold much fear when the zombies crawl near
And emerge from the soft, marshy ground.

I don't ever shake when I hold out a stake
As a vampire looks into my eyes.
And I don't ever tremble when lights that resemble
A spaceship appear in the skies.

But there's one thing that terrifies me, frightens and scarifies me:
Not zombie, nor monster nor ghost.
But it makes my bones shiver, my heart quake and quiver -
Losing you is what I fear the most.

'Nicer' Poems

Right! After all that horrid stuff
I think you've probably had enough
Of monsters who are all around:
Up in the air and underground;
Of oddly, weirdly, strangely things:
Biggle, quag and squorkle-plings;
Disgusting things, of going, "Yuck!"
Of talking about body muck;
Of animals that only do
Disgusting things like fart and poo;
Of being frightened half to death,
And fearing this is your last breath.
I'm going to give you quite a lot
Of poems which are nasty not,
So here's a few good humoured rhymes
(I only mention bum five times).

A disappointing park

I've travelled for so many miles to come here to this park.
I left when it was barely light and now it's nearly dark.
I'm very disappointed with this so called 'leisure' place,
For all I've found are more like me and one big empty space.

And so we are all sat here wondering what on Earth to do.
The others are just sulking for they've come a long way too.
I haven't seen a swing or seesaw, roundabout or slide.
I think that the park owners mean to take us for a ride.

Oh! Here come my four humans, laughing loudly - what's so funny?
In they get and one says, "What a day - well worth the money!"
It's alright for you, I think, *but not much fun for me.*
Humans are so selfish and, I guess, they'll always be.

They clean us and they polish us and sometimes name us too.
And then they leave us in the 'park' and go off to the zoo.
And so we head off home again - a long drive in the dark.
And I still can't understand how they can call this a CAR PARK.

Give the dinosaurs one more chance

Ice caps melting,
Hard rains pelting.
There's a hole up in the sky.
I wonder if the dinosaurs
Should have another try.

Boat or ship?

Why is a boat not a ship?
Why is a ship not a boat?
Both of them go in the water.
Both of them usually float.

I've asked many sailors the question,
But none of them seemed to know when
Boats become ships and ships become boats.
I'm going to ask you once again.

Why is a boat not a ship?
Why is a ship not a boat?
I've sent petty officers letters
And this is what each of them wrote:

A boat is a ship when it's big.
A ship is a boat when it's small.
But other than that they admitted,
They didn't know the answer at all.

But why is a boat not a ship?
And why is a ship not a boat?
The officers had no idea
So I sent the Commander a note.

The Commander arrived here one morning
In a very posh car with a flag.
He told me to mind my own business
And then disappeared in his Jag.

The ghost in the Post Office

The ghost in the Post Office asked to be sent
Second class to the Island of Wight.
But they should have known better -
When they opened the letter
He haunted them all through the night.

The bad fairy

You don't need to open the window
For the fairy of teeth to come in.
She floats through the glass on a light beam
And flies to your bed on the wind.
On your pillow she lands like a feather
And she magics a penny so bright.
She exchanges the tooth for her money
And then disappears into the night.

But if you leave open your window,
Then the bad fairy might just get through.
She can't float through glass on a light beam
And swims through the air like it's glue.
On your pillow she'll land like an anvil,
And she'll push you out onto the floor.
She'll steal all the money donated
By the fairy that came there before.

She'll mess up your room in an instant
And leave you all tangled in sheets,
Then swim with her cash to the window
(And for her that's a difficult feat).
So remember, don't open your window
When the fairy of teeth makes her claim,
Unless your room's very untidy -
Then just say that the bad fairy came.

Never go to an apprentice dentist

Teresa McLeaf had very sharp teeth.
She used them for crunching on rocks.
But her lazy old dentist
Employed an apprentice
And now she can only chew socks.

Junior McSpooner

Junior McSpooner was a serial mooner -
Got his bum out whenever he could.
He thought it was funny to show off his money,
But we all know he'll come to no good.

One day, whilst out mooning, a man was ballooning
So silently over his head.
He had a big gun and was out just for fun,
Hunting squongeese to shoot them all dead.

Now, squongeese can't fly, though they try and they try,
But a foot from the ground and they fall,
For they're related to pigs but are three times as big,
Not connected to goose birds at all.

A distinguishing feature of this piggy like creature
Is that, when it bends downwards to eat,
Its head at the back grows a really big crack
That looks just like a young human's seat.

I expect that you know where this story will go
And the end will not be a surprise,
But it's rather amusing to think of me choosing
A finale where young Junior dies.

So the man out ballooning above Junior mooning,
His gun poised and ready to boom,
Mistook Junior's bum for a squongoose's mum
And that blast signalled poor Junior's doom.

Like most of these tales that involve fateful males
There's a moral that's bound to ensue -
If you drop down your pants there's a pretty good chance
That a man with a gun will get you.

A space log

If I found a twig on Mars
I surely would be famous.
A twig from Mars is better
Than a big log from Uranus.

The Mummy awakens

The Mummy raised its head and stared,
From its long night now awakened.
The explorers looked extremely scared,
Each shivering and shaking.
The sheets wound round its body tight;
A moan came from its lips
And, from its timeless resting place,
Its aged body slipped.
They'd climbed into the Mummy's tomb,
Up darkened steps of plight,
Carrying their gifts of thanks,
Preparing for the rite.
The Mummy staggered forwards,
Arms outstretched, its waking done.
The explorers raised their gifts and cried,
"Happy birthday, Mum!"

Knickers

There are knickers on the washing line -
I think they are my mum's.
I didn't know there were so many
Different kinds of bums.
Some need great big knickers -
Just like tents but without pegs.
And some need really baggy ones
Which hang over their legs.
Some require thin bits of string
For hardly any bum.
But how do all those knickers
Fit the one bum of my mum?

The Saurus

If those dinosaurus
Had Roget's Thesaurus
They would have writ storus
And morus, like mens.

But they had volcanoes
Instead (such a shamoes)
And very small brainoes,
And no ink for pens.

So those prehistoric
Beasts didn't get faric
Until that big staric
Exploded on Earth.

And, with a great roarus,
That promised thesaurus
Was to be no morus
Until Roget's birth.

How my great, great granddad died

The day my great, great granddad died
He wasn't sliding down a slide;
He wasn't swinging on a swing;
He was hardly doing anything;
He wasn't on a roundabout;
He was very nearly doing nowt.
But he left his own personal mark
Upon a seat within the park -
My great, great granddad died whilst he
Was sitting on the lavatory.

Evil square

Evil square
Standing there
Equal sides and angles

Polygon
Not much on
Talking to rectangles

Circle rolls
Past them all
Doesn't want to stop

Evil square
Sees him there
Gobbles circle up

Polygon
Says, "That's not on."
And so the square replies:

"He was a-round
Too often and
He never could choose sides."

Out my window

From my bed I can gaze out my window
And look at the stars in the sky.
And somewhere tonight in that darkness
A planet is going to die.

And somewhere tonight on that planet
There's an alien boy that will be
Looking out of his own bedroom window
And wishing that he was a me.

A little festive mistake

I saw a little Santa in a teeny little sleigh,
Pulled by some little reindeer that had flown a little way.
They had some little presents for the little girls and boys.
They left some little paw prints and they made a little noise.
They stopped on little houses and they stayed a little while,
And little Santa hopped right off and gave a little smile.
Then down the little chimney with a little, "Ho! Ho! Ho!"
He pulled his little sack and waved a little cheerio.
A little after midnight little Santa came back out,
And flew a little closer and I had a little doubt.
I felt a little stupid, on this little Christmas day.
None of them were little, just a little way away.

The end of the world

When the end of the world comes and knocks on my door,
Do you think I could ask for just five minutes more?
For I'm bound to be writing down words at the time
And I'd like to be able to finish my rhyme.

Some interesting facts about Mike Lucas…

- He lives in a house…
- …that used to be pink but is now yellow…
- …with one wife, two children, two four legged cats, one three legged cat and a hamster…and a slug which lives half way up the kitchen window…and sometimes a few fleas.
- He used to live in Switzerland with his family and three cats. When he returned back home some nice ladies flew the cats back in their own private aeroplane. They're all buried in the back garden now (the cats, that is, not the nice ladies).
- He practises tae kwon do. He also runs a lot. This is good because he isn't very good at tae kwon do, so he can run away instead.
- He lives in a different world from most people. Sometimes he has to come out of that world to do boring things like going to work and being ill and talking to people.
- In the world where he lives, anything can happen. Anything at all! It all depends on what he is thinking about at the time. For example, once he was thinking about what would happen if a cow with no previous flying experience had to land a helicopter…He only just escaped from the field, where he was counting blades of grass, in time. Alas, the sheep who were playing golf at the time weren't so lucky!
- He tries not to have too many bad thoughts.
- He has been to the moon where it was cold.
- Oh, and another thing – he's quite mad, you know.
- Moo!

www.gingercatpublishing.co.uk